CURSE ME BY YOUR NAME

BY

PHRIQUE

<u>Trigger Warning</u>

This is a work of literary nonsense (of the highest caliber) that depicts the afterlife of an infamous legendary icon with a name that hoes just can't keep out of their mouths. She works hard, and she plays...well...just read the damned story, you'll see. There's no more **BLOOD** and **SENSELESS VIOLENCE** than I would imagine is in a typical wage slave/office job.

(Hell if I know, couldn't be meeee.)

Regardless, **36 WHOLE ASS YOUTHS DIE** while Ms. Mary earns her paycheck. So if that's not your cup of tea, or it might prompt a call to HR, it's probably best to avoid this one, Helen. Let's give Sandra a break, for once. Mayhaps I could interest you in something a little lighter. Have you ever had any impure thoughts about Ronald McDonald?

xoxo,

Phrique

Phrique

Phrique

(Say it out loud, I dare ya!)

Dedicated to:

Kids with parents who gave them bad names, literally. You didn't deserve that orthographic atrocity of a first name, lil' Brentistopher. Your parents were just mad that they got stuck with shit like Henry or fuckin' Roberta. Bless their hearts.

Contents

Chapter 1

A Grout Stain Most Stubborn

I let out a frustrated sigh and do my dumb little stretches during the transfer. I roll my shoulders, loosen my jaw up a bit, and stretch my nimble fingers outward. *It's the strains and sprains that get you, ya know.* I fan out my claws in preparation, feeling their heft as they file against each other, honing their edges as if they could get any sharper. I float into the inky blackness.

The stench of accrued urine makes my nose scrunch up. Thankfully, my mordant red lip gloss has a pleasant merlot scent to help mask the pungency that has become a common occupational hazard: *boy bathrooms.*

Through the back of the shimmering portal, I see four snickering twerps, three no more than fourteen years old. My summoner is the younger, quivering boy about to seal his fate. Gone are my reservations of compassion for the living, even those who haven't had much time on earth to do so. The little one, who looks like he couldn't be more than...twelve? I can see the innocence in his hesitation. A rationality that isn't usually harnessed in someone his age, certainly not his gender. If only Kharlo knew that he was only two words away from becoming a brilliant cardiologist with a practice in Hoboken *or* a stubborn grout stain on this tiled floor.

A pregnant pause and an intensity is floating in the already thick, humid air. The lone air freshener/night light is barely doing either of its jobs well. A wave of horripilation sweeps over the young men who would never see the *joys* of adulthood. They can't place it, but they can feel my presence. My sickly sweet scent floats on the stagnant air, lighting up cautionary pathways in their still-forming grey matter that they've yet to recognize. *Shame*.

One boy senses the fragrance of his own funeral arrangements. His eyes dart to the silhouette I've allowed him and only him to see. My nostrils flare in anticipation. I love a *will-they-won't-they* moment, don't you? Ronaldo appears to gather his thoughts, pushing past his hard-wired neanderthal inner workings. Little man is about to save the day, it seems, as I begin my retreat. I got all dolled up for noth—

"**Bloody Mary,**" whispers Kharlo, in a frail tone.

The last words that he will ever utter, unless you count screams powerful enough to shred his vocal cords. I might have shed a tear if I hadn't finally perfected that wing on my cat eye, for once.

Well, I think, *ready or not, time to show off that wing tip.*

I dive through the surface of the rippling mirror with my claws extended, ready to soak in all the life force they can extract. Teenage boy screams reach a fevered pitch as I rake my talons through Matteo, carving grooves in his ribs as the lungs behind them suck in their last sopping breath. I was aiming for the one who summoned me, but Kharlo had collided with his cousins in the commotion before they broke out into stooge-like alarm.

Boys will be boys.

I obscure myself as the blood absorbs through my pallid skin, invigorating me to carry on the carnage that was my calling. It was just the pick-me-up I needed to grab Ronaldo with my free hand. His cousins watch his flailing body float above their cowering faces. *I'm not always such a sourpuss.* I'll admit, my hand exploding through Ronaldo's chest cavity, spraying the boys with bits of gore and bone, brought a smirk to my face. Which I let them finally see as I materialized and cleaved my claws down, bisecting Ronaldo; pelting Kharlo and Juni with his adorable little vital organs.

By now, the boys were slipping and sliding on the slick blood rink I made just for them to play on. Screaming for Mrs. Pelayo, who was at work and would ultimately blame herself for the mess, *once she regained consciousness*. The same mess, the realtor, Mrs. Cartwright, would be damning once she saw the nightmare that was the grout, *months from now*. So much heartache, so much wasted potential, all on account of man's morbid curiosity with the afterlife. Instead of just living life to the fullest, knowing their time was finite, they see fit to summon demons. Entities whose very names forewarn: *there will be blood*, like that's a given.

The folly of man, I ponder wistfully as my pronged phalanges skewer Kharlo's eyeballs to the rattling door. Juni shrieks as the remnants of one less cardiologist in the world shower down upon him, followed by his lifeless, quivering body. Juni's hands pull at the blood-slicked door handle, but the pile of cooling bodies in front of the threshold impedes him.

I lift him by his collar, my razor-sharp claws dotting his skin as I decide his fate. I could let him live. I haven't let a frantic *final girl* survive in a while. Someone to recount the tale of how they survived; what they saw; the screams; the nightmares; the sleepless nights, knowing no one wanted to believe the truths they prattled on regarding what truly lurked behind the looking glass. But was it wise to entrust this to little stuttering, yammering Juni?

I stare into Juni's frenzied eyes, allowing a hint of illumination to shine through the other side of the mirror so he has the full story to tell. I deem him a good investment. The childlike joy is literally dying in his eyes before me, but I know my legend is safe in his blood-caked hands. This would scar him enough never to be fully right again, but not go catatonic on me. *Hopefully.*

I need to get my believer count up, dammit. I would cross my fingers if I weren't holding him close enough that the stench of rotting death on my breath overcomes him. My toes dip back into the silver pool of the mirror as I begin to cut and run. Juni's eyes grow larger than I thought humanly possible as he watches me disappear into the mercurial ripples, thinking I would drag him in with me.

Silly child, I think as I begin my descent and slam his forehead into the spiderwebbed mirror I leave behind. He crumples onto the counter as his unconscious body is showered by mirror shards.

Go forth Juni, plant that seed of fear for me to sew. Let me cultivate that shred of curiosity until the day that cat grows curious enough to summon a cheap thrill. So that I can claim another, bathe in their essence, and lessen my sentence. For not all curious cats get the axe, some of us just learn there's more to this world than meets the eye.

Chapter 2

Everyone Hates the Tooth Fairy

The humming fluorescents sting my light-sensitive corneas enough to make them tear up. The putrid stench wasn't helping. Pearl cooked fish in the fucking microwave again. Why don't the fairy tales elaborate on how inconsiderate and passive-aggressive the fae are? We all have to suffer because the Tooth Fairy decides to go pescatarian? Ever since the bone elemental got her Disney princess pixie glow-up, all she cares about is how she looks in her athleisure. I preferred her old look, though I'm sure I'm in the minority. The few kids who saw her true form, when they opened their eyes before she completed their transaction, disagree. Those who lived long enough to be institutionalized anyway.

I flutter the moisture from my eyes as I feel the last drops of Kharlo soak into my pale skin. *Or maybe that's Ronaldo?* I ponder this as I take the long way across the tan berber-carpeted office floor. The last thing anyone wants is to have a banshee talk their ear off. The few banshees that were left, at least.

There's a blinking email notification on my desktop screen after I log in, zapping the last bit of energy I extracted from my previous appointment. A flap of bloody pancreas dislodges from under my nail, splatting on my otherwise spotless workstation. I eye it with disdain as I open the email and see what the rest of my day will be like.

Time for another annual performance evaluation. Has it been a year already?

I slide my headset on and stare at my solemn reflection in my screen. I'm supposed to be making sure my eye makeup didn't smear, but the depressed looking ghoul staring back at me seemed like she had bigger problems. I connect to the Zoom meeting, already in progress.

"Well, look who decided to join us. *Privet Masha*."

Only the Baba Yaga can call me Masha; everyone else knows I will turn them into spurting Pez dispensers at even the thought. Pearl, with her blonde bob, is winking at me, or perhaps she's just blinking glitter out of her eye between bites. The lady in white, La Llorona, is sobbing as usual—on mute—thankfully. Always the gentleman, Mordrake faces away from the camera, letting his prettier visage take this meeting. She's the only one who has anything interesting to say, anyway. Slenderman—or his elongated limbs, at least—begin to glitch in and out of his screen. *That guy knows how to commit to the bit.*

"*Masha*, we were just discussing Daniel's success and what we could emulate from him."

Daniel Robitaille's name appeared on a vacant, darkened box on our screens.

"Oh? Is Daniel here? Is *Candyman* not too *Hollywood* for us anymore?" I let out, already knowing the answer.

The Baba Yaga's kind expression grimaced. She pulled her thin lips into an extended frown and shook her silver-bunned head at her camera.

"Masha, don't be like that. You could learn a thing or two from Daniel. He may be your junior, but look how far he's gone," said a wilted Yaga.

"Sure, give me a movie deal and a reboot, and watch how quickly my numbers skyrocket. Meanwhile, I still show up to meetings. Even off a fresh kill." I spit snidely, proudly flicking a bit of gelatinous gray matter out of my hair.

"When was his last kill?" I ask, "and don't say the box office, Pearl, unless you want to be picking your latest acquisitions up off the floor."

That was going to be an HR (Humanoid Resources) write-up, but I couldn't care less.

On cue, Pearl began to choke on her scaly snack.

Good. I hope a whole fish carcass is perforating her larynx.

Her baby doll blue eyes water as she clearly is about to asphyxiate on whatever is lodged in her throat. Her pretty new face, complete with a sculpted jawline, contorts and hollows. Bone shards crackle beneath her low-cut sweater, slicing from newly formed rips in her beautifully tanned chest and neck.

"There she is!," I cackle, almost falling out of my office chair when a tiny, overcooked fish bone flies out of her overextended jaw. Her blindingly white quills pull back inside her damaged facade, and she clears her throat.

"I'm going to take my 15," Pearl said quickly, exiting the meeting.

"Let's all take 15, *deti*." Yaga decrees. "Mary, my office."

The Zoom meeting closes, and I'm left staring at my scowling reflection in my blank screen, yet again.

I make a pit stop at the Lady's restroom, washing my hands and dabbing at the marrow stain on my otherwise all black ensemble. I'm officially stalling. I know Yaga is going to grind my bones into porridge for this one. *I don't know what's been going on with me lately, I just...*

I look into the mirror and stare into my silver eyes. *Say it*, I coax myself. Self-reflection is kinda my thing, but I just couldn't quite put my talon on it. So why not consult my mirror dimension self? She always appears like she's dying to clue me in on what she sees that I can't. Watching her, watching me, giving me the up-and-down as she shakes her head. *I will never get my wing tip that precise ever again.* A knot of doubt forms in my belly like a maelstrom of nervous energy, as I involuntarily shake my head as well. We bring our faces closer to the mirror's surface. She begins to speak, and "You're heart's just not in it anymore" spills from our lips simultaneously.

Before I have time to roll that around in my skull, the bathroom door swings open. The harpy with the pixie cut from accounting walks in. The company's unofficial gossip: her wings should be jealous of all the flapping her little button beak got to do. I stifle a giggle.

Oh Mary, that was horrible. No more Friends reruns for you.

Circe sidles up and uses the sink next to me, blinking her beady little eyes.

"Oh, Mary, I love that lip color. It looks so enchanting on you."

I do my best to make my grin look real, in the mirror at least, while I dig in my purse for the tube of lipstick.

"It's called Sang de Enfante."

"Let me guess," Circe pauses, "vintage?"

From anyone else, I wouldn't question this comment, but Circe was known for purposely ruffling feathers. Luckily for her, I just fed and remembered that I had absent-mindedly left the lipstick on my bathroom counter at home.

"You know it," I muster with the thinnest veneer of tolerance I can, as I reach my hand through the mirror and pull the silver-capped lipstick back through the rippling surface.

"Now I just need to stop leaving it everywhere, before I lose it," I add before I reapply.

Circe watches the color glide on my lips as I pout and pucker.

"They don't make 'em like that anymore, that's for sure," she says while pausing her sweater vest preening to watch me in the mirror. My reflection winks at her. I chuckle, pop the tube back in my purse, and do a final turn in the mirror.

"Good luck with Yaga." She coos as I head for the exit.

I could probably use it.

Chapter 3

<u>Baba Knows Best</u>

I buoyantly trudge my way to the Baba Yaga's office; my Green Mile. The black-eyed children avert their gaze, pretending to focus on delivering mail as I hover past them. The whole floor was eerily silent besides the sickly whispers coming from the other side of Mordrake's coifed, yet malformed head. I could see why Edward cursed his conjoined-terror-twin's incessant gibbering. There are only so many vapid Instagram inspirational quotes one can tolerate before *anyone* would go mad. I linger in front of Yaga's door a beat before I raise a sweaty fist to knock, when the door opens on its own.

"Hang in theereee" whispers Mordrake's demoness twin, as I enter.

An 18th-century Russian settee whisks around me, scooping me up in its plush ivory silk and bringing me toward Yaga's mahogany desk. *The solid gold chicken feet were a little kitsch, but who didn't like to bring a little bit of home with them?*

Yaga was turned away from me in her leather wheeled throne. My stall tactics didn't seem to have calmed her any.

"Tea, Mary?" she said as a teapot with a cup and saucer hovered in front of me. I eyed the rustic china suspiciously.

"Maybe once we get past all this Mary business," I say. "And maybe when I find out what kind of tea it is."

The accouterments quietly place themselves back on her desk. The Baba Yaga turns in her chair with a knowing smirkle on her face.

"Just chamomile, Masha." She shook her head and tut-tutted me.

"If I wished ill of you, I would just make it so that all the mirrors in the world broke at once." Her smile was genuine, her grandmotherly face warming as she sipped her tea. I let my guard down, relaxing my tensed muscles enough to sink into the lush upholstery.

"My Masha, what am I to do with you?"

Floating her cup back to its saucer, she brought her seasoned hands together in a steeple in front of the white, billowing sleeves of her traditional red sarafan.

"You are one of our senior agents. The *deti* are in awe of your numbers. I so hoped that after we broke away from B.O.O. (the Boogie Oogie Objective) that you would have crossed over to management. It would get you out of the field and into a more...*relaxed environment*. Maybe that's something we should perhaps look into?"

She materialized in front of me and lifted my chin with her pointy finger nail.

"Have you been feeling well? You look...peaked." Nesting my face in her hands.

"I just fed. This is as rosy as I'm going to get, Yaga."

I fought to keep my face from cracking into a stifled laugh. Baba Yaga did one more cursory scan over me before the worry washed away and her warm grin returned. She let her hands fall to my shoulders.

"So if it isn't in here," she tapped from my shoulders down to my arms rambunctiously. "Then it's in here." She said, pointing through my jet black hair to my head.

She's right.

The aged witch who had become like family to me disappeared, but her voice still boomed through the space.

"Of course I'm right. I'm always right." Her voice returned to her desk, where she reappeared.

"So your heart's not in it. Who's is? I think the only still-beating heart in this office is Sandra's, and that thing's probably the size of a microwave."

I start to respond, but pause, processing her admission of knowing things about myself that I had only learned minutes ago.

"I hear everything. I know everything. I know you."

She leans back in her chair and telekinetically picks up her tea.

"Get out of your head. Get into your heart. See what makes it go pitter-patter. Let's adopt a new credo. Listen to the monster in your heart, not the monster in your head. Ok?"

I can't help but smile and accept the cup of herbaceous tea pouring in front of me.

"Maybe Sandra can pull her weight in HR and get you some extra PTO, too."

I take a sip and feel the golden brew warm my rigored limbs, nodding in appreciation.

"Then maybe we can talk about you coming to the dark side."

Her eyes creased into mischievous, wrinkled triangles, and a mephistophelian grin crackled across her face.

"Management."

Baba chuckled at her own joke.

"I'd like more women in positions of power here, show these old fuddy-duddies what D.I.L. F. (the Department of Infamous Lore Folk) really stands for."

I almost snort tea out of my nose trying to dislodge my caught breath.

"I told you, Yaga, D.I.L.F. has a completely different meaning now. One of my first managerial tasks would be to come up with a totally different company name."

The Baba Yaga threw her hands up in the air, while her cup and saucer stayed hovering in place.

"Ah, phooey, I can't keep up with these little zombies. Always with their noses millimeters from their phones, when they should be listening for bumps in the night. No ambitions. No will to live. It's no wonder our numbers look so bad in the first quarter. All these kids want to do is vape, eat Tide pods, and hot chips until they die from one or the other." She adds, shaking her head.

I rise from the floating settee.

"Speaking of Tide Pods, I need to get this to the dry cleaners. I never get there before they close, and the owner's husband doesn't seem to appreciate it when I show up after hours."

Baba snapped her fingers, and the door to her en suite bathroom opened.

"Take the back way. Don't tell them I let you clock out early," she says with a wink. I leave my cup and saucer on her desk, gliding towards her executive bathroom. I'm halfway through her vanity mirror when she yells,

"Oh! It's Sandra's 80k tomorrow! Cake in the break room!"

I flutter my phalanges to her with my reflection and spirit away to *The Lone Sock* dry cleaners.

Chapter 4

A Meet-cute Made in Hell

I made it just in time, thankful that the owner was closing today. Her husband was such a hot head. Kuchisake-onna, the slit-mouthed woman, and I go way back. She asks how business is as I change out of my work outfit. I throw on the same black ensemble I'm picking up.

Don't judge. After 400 years in the biz, I know what works and what doesn't.

We laugh about how many foolish men answered her question wrong, compared to how many women got it right. She's just as beautiful as ever, though I'm smart enough to not relay that to her directly.

On the way home, I visit a few old haunts. Seeing my old work friend put a little pep in my proverbial step. I float past my threshold, still in high spirits. I decide to conclude my night by putting on some old jazz to begin my skincare routine. The music notes calm me while they float in the air in my perceived condo. The floors, ceilings, and walls all exist (*or do they?*) as they fade out into nothingness.

Hey buddy, I'm telling the story here. If you would like to get deep into the quantum physics of supernatural subletting in inter-dimensionally liminal spaces, we'll have to save that for another time.

I pull my hair back into a top knot, regarding my prominent features in my bathroom mirror. I proceed to daub said features with Dead Sea mud and stare off into my own reflection as the mask works its magic.

The predicament with mirrors being your *thing* for so long is that they become your double-edged sword. I'm a pretty observant entity, but there's such a thing as being over-observant, too. My eyes focus on a fine line sliced across my forehead. My thinking line, *my overthinking lines,* my judgment lines, my *this is why you're single lines.* I feel my mood deflate, and I wonder if there's any wine in the fridge. Yaga's words echo through my head; probably directly from her at this very moment.

"Listen to the monster in your heart, not the monster in your head."

I watch the tension melt off my mirror dimension's face while the mud mask stays intact. Just like that, I quiet my inner critique, my self-saboteur.

That felt pretty good, actually.

I rinse off the mask and dry my face, noticing it's still pretty early. What should I do with my night? Binge some SkinWalker Ranch? Dive into my horror library and read some non-fiction (fiction) about my friends and loved ones?

I change into my 'round-the-house catsuit and throw my phone in my robe pocket when I feel it vibrate. I never logged out of my conjuration receiver after I left Baba's office.

To my surprise, I have a possible summoning. It's late, but not too late.

It's probably some cliche sorority sacrificing their pledges to stay young for a few more years.

The location is not far from me, but then again, no place is far from me in the mirror-verse.

Nope, I'm still not getting into it, just listen.

I'm hesitant, but curious. There's a little spark where my motivation used to be.

Who doesn't like a little overtime? Might as well strike while I have the spare energy, I think, as I swap my robe for a hoodie and a dab of lip gloss.

Then the next thing I know, I'm touching my mirror's surface staring into some conjurer's bathroom. A cheery, light space. Very pink.

It's cute, just...not for me.

I hear music in the distance. Sad vocals drift in from the other room, but I can't angle myself to see into it. I get close enough to almost see my breath on the back of the mirror.

You know, if I had breath.

A ghostly pale apparition catches my eye. A girl, a young woman with a lavender and black bob, in a t-shirt and pastel pajama shorts, walks in front of the mirror and turns to stare right at me. I'm taken aback. I've never experienced such a jaw-dropping marvel before today. Yet, here she is. Kyoko, twenty-six, college student, #sad-girl. *Whatever that means. Sometimes it felt like the gremlins in data entry just made up information as they went along.*

I curiously watch as she climbs up on the counter and sits, placing her feet in the sink. She takes a swig of a *Jamaican Me Crazy* wine cooler and continues to look at me/herself in the mirror. The beautiful specimen is staring harshly at her own reflection. A little part of me wishes I could take some of that steely gaze so she wouldn't have to. I know that look all too well.

Her pillowy pink lips are still slick from her fruity drink of choice. The skin around her big brown eyes are just as pink and a bit puffy. There's a burdened malaise in her stare that hits a little too close to home.

I am captivated. I know this girl. I was this girl. So many eons ago. Yet not so long ago, not so lavender. Being only number seventeen in the long line of Bloody Mary successors, I hold all their prior experiences and knowledge. *Whether I like it or not.* Maybe that's why I can feel both four hundred and thirty years old at the same time. It's more *Handbook for the Recently Deceased* fine print that I'm not at liberty to discuss.

I'm lost in Kyoko's sorrowful gaze. I can feel myself getting choked up, feeling closer than ever to a human emotion since before the world was introduced to indoor plumbing. Imagine the fun I had surfacing in poorly ventilated privies to eviscerate some-

"**Bloody Mary**"

Kyoko's angelically sad voice sucks the air out of my non-corporeal lungs. Both hearing it for the first time, but also becoming unbearably apprehensive at its implications.

No no no no no. I beg her. *Stop this.*

My eyes are trained on her. I can see her black manicured fingers reaching for something out of my periphery. I already know that she's palming the freed blade from the box cutter, and I already know why. I don't know what's come over me. This is against every protocol that I know, but my non-functioning heart, the thing I just started listening to, is screaming at me to INTERVENE. I can't get a read on her fate or where her life may go if she doesn't go forward with this pact, but I know her future will be bright. I know she will be someone's everything, someday. She just needs to back away from the mirror and keep her mouth shut.

She holds the razor in one shaky hand and brings the other to her forehead. She sniffles, letting tears cascade down her rosy cheeks. Even her ugly crying face is beautiful to me. She wipes the tears away and places her wet hand on the mirror. My hollow chest feels like it's about to burst with all the things I want to say to her. The knowledge that I want to impart to her. I want to tell her how much lonelier it is on this side. How much she would miss the tiniest things she takes for granted now. All lost because she thinks this is her only choice.

I wipe the trickle of crimson that runs down my cheek and place my hand against the paper-thin, yet impenetrable space between us. This is the one loophole that I can't circumnavigate. I can't come in unless I'm summoned. The contract is ironclad, written in blood. They do their part, then I do mine. No hard feelings. No love lost. No survivors.

I can feel her heart beating through the pane of glass; I can hear her thoughts.

I don't want to die alone. That's all I ask.

My heart breaks into a thousand pieces. A sob escapes my throat that rattles the pane between us into a series of pops and sharp snaps. We both watch as the mirror shatters and the radiating cracks slice into our open palms. I watch her gasp in confusion as our hands feel fused on the spot, until a jolt of pain makes us pull them back in unison. An ethereal light emanates from the cracks, like tiny lightning bolts energizing the pooled blood on either side of the glass. We both look at our palms and watch the amalgamation seep into our wounds and knit our flesh back together, thinking before we both pass out.

I'm going to be in such deep shit tomorrow.

Chapter 5

Let HR Handle It

There are a lot more mirror-commuting entities than you'd think. That's why the conjuration receivers were imperative. Scanning the collective so we don't have any more double-booking ordeals on jobs. It also cuts down on the ol' fraternity prank where they try to pit one of us against the other to see who wins.

I won every time, by the way, but that's beyond the point. Where is my brain this morning? That was the most vivid dream I've had in what feels like centuries. Come to think of it...I don't think I can dream.

I reflect through the lobby's full-length mirror into the D.I.L.F. building. Luckily, there wasn't much of a line, but that means I'm even more late than I expected. The security check queue allows me to finish shoving my foot into my shoe. I look at the clock in the marbled lobby and see it's three minutes til.' I was about to ask what the delay was when I noticed the tumult at the security kiosk and the line of people. Circe—my favorite harpy—is front and center, warbling away. They must be preparing for another nest raid. That chick will never learn.

I get waved through and take a huge sigh of relief, having made it just in time. I head for the elevator, where Cornelius—the unicorn from Grants & Wishes on the 7th floor—holds the door for me. I'm about to step on when I swear I hear my name being called. I push past Cornelius' horn, careful not to take out an eye, when a determined voice calls my name for a second time. My skin prickles as my conjuration receiver goes off in my purse. I grit my teeth and prepare for detonation. My claws engorge, and black blood seeps from my eyes. Electricity courses through the air as Cornelius and the djinn twins all scream, "Whoa! Whoa!" as the bounding security guard practically skids into the elevator with us.

"What?!" The hellhound artlessly barks as he is given death stares by the elevator passengers. "Oh, yeah, my bad." He says, tucking his whiskered chin and thrusting his hand in my face. "I think this belongs to you," he says, revealing my *vintage* lipstick in his paw. I lower my hackles and take it back, tucking it in my purse pocket.

"It had your scent, I just-I-I-" he stammered, taking a step back out of the elevator.

With the tension dissipated and everything retracted, I smile and lean closer to him as the door begins to slide closed jerkily.

"Good boy," I whisper, making his blazing eyes light up before the elevator closes and whisks us up to our respective floors.

I exchange pleasantries with the dual flames, Azar and Zara, before I'm let off onto the 6th floor to the sound of painful wails and pandemonium.

It was hump day after all.

I walk past the printed-out banner in reception that reads, "Happy 80k Kills Sandra!" My stomach already aches. Not another cake. We still had leftover cannonball-themed birthday cake in the break room fridge from the Headless Horseman's birthday. *How gauche.* The Wendigo already had blood sugar issues as it is; let's not put him back in an early grave. I decide to keep my frivolous platitudes to myself for once; surprisingly, since:

1. I don't eat.

2. I'm in a good mood still, considering I'm not entirely sure what the heaven happened last night.

Just as I'm about to turn the corner to absentmindedly head to my desk, I'm cut off by the bratty kids from our on-site childcare services on the ground floor. Holda, their *Gingerbread Ma'am*, chases after them with sheet music, giving me an apologetic, flustered grimace.

Want to know what keeps death-dealing revenants and souls of the damned up at night? Kids. Kids singing. Total fucking nightmare fuel.

They are really going all out for Sandra. *Good for her.* I can't wait till I get to my 80k someday, daydreaming as I go the opposite way.

Suddenly, a cold, bony hand stops me in my tracks. The tooth fairy's over-familiar gesture successfully pulls me from my dissociative automaticity, just long enough to witness a screaming child being ripped in two by teeth the size of traffic cones. The blur of violence is black, and white, and red all over as blood splashes my unsuspecting coworkers. Pearl still has her hand on my chest for some reason, restraining me, when I notice she's using her pinky nail to pick something out of her teeth.

Always the charmer.

We both watch the carnage unfold as Sandra's powerful jaws clamp around the torsos of two more kids with a deafening snap. Her gold doorknocker earrings gave a distracting little shimmer before the sound of their bones cracking brought me back. The crunch of their frail little bodies snapping under the pressure like a handful of chopsticks gets drowned out when the sewer 'gator began her death roll, tussling what's left of their mangled corpses around like bloodied doll parts. Our leviathan HR supervisor throws her gargantuan body in a spin, causing her cute little novelty celebration sombrero to fall off while she takes out cubicles and desks left and right. Pearl finally dislodged an ossicle bone from her teeth and spat it demurely in her hand. I cut my eyes at her incredulously as she popped it back in her mouth and chewed away. *Pescatarian, my ass.*

"Sorry," she said, sounding surprisingly sincere for once, "that was bothering me."

I raise my eyebrows and nod, watching Sandra's muscular tail whip a cluster of kids into the stone walls. Two of them were impaled and gored on the rows of coat hooks that the Crooked Man requested last month. The others were jettisoned through the inner-office windows, sending their glass-encrusted bodies into conference room C.

"So...what's up with Sandra?" I ask, eying the few cowering kids screaming for their parents in the corner.

"WELL," Pearl begins.

Here we go.

"Brigitte got a cake for her 80k."

"So?" I say.

Our local bog witch loved playing party planner—just no bonfires.

"Sooo," the tooth fairy responded, extra irksomely, "Sandra has a gluten allergy." Pearl put her hands on her bony hips. "Brigette didn't check the food allergy list." She shook her head. "I would be pissed too."

"Well, at least Brigitte is trying to course correct," I say as the bog witch releases the glowing protection impetus from around herself and the few remaining sniveling kids. She snapped her neck in our direction and levitated our way. I recoiled and stepped back, putting my hands up in surrender.

No more hexes for me, thank you very much.

"I know I did *not* hear my name come out of that bear trap you call a mouth, Pearl." Brigitte sassed, landing in front of us. I hated to see strong, independent women bicker, but it was about time Pearl got her teeth rattled.

Pearl was visibly offended, pulling her over-plumped lips tight in annoyance.

"I'm not trying to do this with you right now, *Brigitte*," Pearl said calmly, but threw in some bite at the end. "Last time management got involved, and I don't want to go through all that again."

Brigitte pursed her lips and raised her eyebrows.

"Well, the head of HR is right that way, but she seems a bit indisposed. This is one time your new tight-ass face won't get you to the front of the line. I know that for true." Brigitte snarled.

I snorted, covering it with a cough, turning towards Sandra, chomping on the last few surviving kids, looking a bit spent.

She just hit 80,016. Such an overachiever, that one.

"This isn't about us, Brigitte! You're just deflecting! How do you not know that Sandra has a gluten intolerance? You two carpool together!" Pearl said with her shoulders heaving angrily.

"Bitch, I put my AirPods in and bring my ass to work like everyone else. I don't have to know everything in this office like your ancient ass does."

"Bitch?! Ancient?! You only wish you could… Oooh." Pearl paused, trying to collect herself while rising protrusions were already pressing against the bone elemental's bronzed skin. Her voice deepened and became gravelly. "Let me stop, before I get ugly."

The bog witch let out a cackle so deep that it shook a stained kid's Air Force One from Sandra's maw.

"Bayyyyybeeeeee," Brigitte clapped her hands in front of her as she stifled her laughter.

"You're about a century past ugly! They've found bog bodies that have aged more gracefully than you."

Shards of glowing razor-sharp bones jutted out from Pearl's face like tusks, slicing through her skin and pulling it like an overstretched Halloween mask. Brigitte's palms began to glow. She stared the contorting sea urchin down hard enough that blood began to leak from her eyes. I stepped back behind the half wall of the blown-out conference room nearest to me, followed by the few survivors on the floor.

Just as the fireworks were about to go off, Baba Yaga's door burst open. A cauldron flew into the space, along with the elder banging a giant wooden spoon on it. The bangs resounded through the bloodied battlefield that just moments before hosted muzak & on-the-clock fantasy football talk. Everyone froze, except Sandra, who was half-heartedly rolling around in the gory sludge near a busted water main.

"I was on a group seance call with Rasputin, and this is when you all decided to cause a ruckus?!" Yaga said, detritus floating around her, returning back the way they were before the brouhaha.

Chairs rolled past Yaga as she stepped closer to Pearl and Brigitte stuck in frozen animation, staring them down hard. Then she noticed a little piece of a kid's shirt on the floor, then a little piece of a kid's shoe, then a little piece of a kid. Her nostrils flared.

She turned to Holda, who stood to face Yaga before she licked her lips and hid a little femur behind her back. Baba Yaga rubbed her sinuses with her wrinkled hands.

"Get Veto up here before we start piecing everyone back together," she said to her invisible secretary. A floating yellow bow tie and a corded phone receiver lifted from the desk next to her office in response.

The sound of jiggling expired condiments from the opening break room fridge door pulled me away from watching the show. La Llorona snagged a piece of birthday cake and closed the door with her hip. I guess it *was* about time to get back to work. Too bad the water main busted above my work area, so it looks like I will be working remotely for a while.

I watched the sputtering water come to an end as Baba Yaga cinched the pipe closed with a clenching of her fist. The small pond on the floor was still spreading, letting loose a small river that crept below me. My eyes fluttered down to it furtively before they doubled back at lightning speed. My reflection was gone, replaced with the sorrowful face of the girl from last night. I couldn't pry my eyes from her pouting lips as she tied her hair up into a messy bun. I glanced back at Yaga, praying she wasn't waiting for the hysterics to die down to call me back in her office.

She was busy pulling the kids off the wall hooks and adding them to the pile, shaking her head, thankfully. By the time I looked back at Kyoko, I saw her capping her lip gloss, and the bathroom went dark.

What the heaven is going on here?

"Baba," a feminine, disembodied male voice rang out, "we've got an issue."

Baba Yaga turned toward the direction of the floating landline and the cute yellow bow tie near her office while she telekinetically held Sandra's massive jaws open.

"What is it, Loot? Spit it out!"

"Veto is on vacation for the week. His daughter's destination wedding, remember?"

Baba Yaga slowly blinked in his direction while she magically pulled the bony stew out from Sandra's gut. The slopping sound of salvaged little fingers and toes resonated in the space as it piled higher.

"Well, can't you call-"

"I called Mr. Graves, too. He's on sabbatical. There are no more necromancers in our network, I'm afraid."

Baba Yaga pursed her lips.

"Of course." She said, sounding exhausted as the last of the pulverized preschooler pulp fell at her feet.

"My kingdom for a private necromancer! Necromancing for money! Any old spell will do!" She yelled frustratedly, shaking her oversized spoon at the sky. "Loot, get Janitorial up here pronto. Tell them we need all shop vacs on deck."

I felt my conjuration receiver vibrate in my purse, like clockwork. I needed to be gone like yesterday. I fish my phone out and silence the notification while it fetches the coordinates for me. I step out of my temporary hiding space and hold my phone out for Baba to see, making the *sorry, I gotta run* face. Her stare softens, and she gives me a nod. I head to the restroom mirror. She returns to her office. We both needed to be anywhere but there.

Chapter 6

Hot Sorority Babes Getting Wet & Wild

Ah, The Kappa Zeta Jones Sorority, I knew it well. I see they've painted since last time. They're going to have to get all new carpet next week. Time to dip into those pledge funds of theirs.

My head already begins to pound as the shrieks and girly giggling worm their way into my ears. It seems that Angela—the house mom snoring away a few feet below the crowing co-eds—never warned them about the fate of their long-forgotten sisters of the 1987 chapter. It must have slipped her mind after all the cognitive processing therapy. I hope she kept her shrink's number handy.

Six jubilant, jostling juveniles are laughing, rolling around a big pink bed. Only one is in her early twenties, and she's barely coherent at this point.

Tiffyneigh would have been the one who got away, the one who was smart enough to get out of the house and run to the nearest emergency station on campus. Unfortunately, she won't even make it off the bed. She's going to be the reason why they're going to have to paint the ceilings below us.

Raspberry Schnapps. *"Not even once"* should be the co-ed's liquor of choice's new slogan.

Bequi, Heighleigh, Tiffyneigh, Amberleigh, Carleigh, and Lux. I cringe. One more and this could have been a fucked up fairytale.

Lux is my conjurer. Praise the Dark Lord. My synapses hurt just trying to figure out how to pronounce half of their names out loud.

Lux is only eighteen, a bright bio student, only talked into joining a sorority to appease her mother and help her come out of her shell.

Way to go Mom.

Lux takes another shot off the tray on the makeup vanity. She's going to need as much liquid courage as she can stomach to push past that stubborn wall of common sense that she banked on for so long. She shudders as the burn leaves her throat and stares into the mirror, directly at me. I raise my eyebrows at the young brunette beauty.

Your move.

Heighleigh and Amberleigh are gyrating on each other, unaware that Bequi and Carleigh put Lux up to this.

"Told you she was too chicken shit to do it," Bequi said in the most grating vocal fry voice known to man, before she knocks back another shot.

"No, she's not," Carleigh coos, "she's just stalling to add to the drama." Both blonde girls laugh and give Lux's shoulders a shake, making her grimace as every cell of her body tells her to desist, to just give up and let them haze her.

"It won't work unless you turn the lights off too!" yells Heighleigh as she fires up TikTok Live and places her phone on her mounted ring light. My reflective eyes light up.

Yessssss, let's give them a show, ladies.

"Hit the lights, Tiff!" Amberleigh yells while she continues to dance to the thumping mumbling *music* playing from the hot pink Bluetooth speaker fixed to the wall. Tiffyneigh groggily pries her eyes from her phone and slurs something about no devil worship allowed in the sorority house. My eyes strain from all the rolling, and my thoughts replay seeing Kyoko, looking better than when I saw her last.

Ugh, can we get this over with? Today ladies?

Tiffyneigh attempts to stand, almost losing her footing twice before she kneels and reaches for the light switch. I watch Lux nervously watching Tiff's hand, and my countdown begins. Lux's childhood fear of the dark ignites, fueling her poor decision-making skills to reach the next level.

"Bloody Mary!"

Lux yells, and the room erupts with screams and laughter. My digits lengthen as I slowly allow the mirror's surface to go translucent. The girls grow silent. The only noise is the annoying percussion of the music. My nails scrape the glass turning all eyes to me.

Showtime.

Lux's eyes water as I break the surface. My claws reach for her cherubic face like a warm embrace as I launch her screaming body out of the chair, and we fly backward. My thumbs skewer her bright green eyes until we hit the wall and I pierce her skull, nailing it to the poster behind her. Several fluids drain out of the new holes I've created, spraying the other girls out of their stunned stupor. Lux hits the floor, jolting the pair nearest to shriek in terror.

Tiffyneigh, broken from her stare, falls back onto the bed just as the dancing TikTok girls are trying to climb over it, hoping to escape. Heigh-leigh and Amberleigh's slippered feet crack three of Tiff's ribs and cave her nose in. She shrieks from the pain and the pressure as the two besties clamor for the door. I stop them in their tracks with two middle fingers applied just under their chins before I rocket their crushed skulls up into the ceiling. Beautiful blooms of red paint the drywall and my glowing white skin before it soaks in to both. Their lifeless bodies fall back to the increasingly reddening carpet and slump against the door, posing for their final selfie in the still recording camera gaze.

I hope Kyoko doesn't try that shit again tonight. I hope I scared the life back into her, for once.

Tiffyneigh is hacking up blood, befuddled, writhing like a stuck turtle. I figure if I am on camera, might as well give 'em the ol' razzle-dazzle. I press my palms together and dive into Lake Tiffyneigh. My talons tear until I feel boxspring. Then I gracefully abduct and part the pickled princess in a red sea with open arms before I pull a back handspring and land perfectly poised.

I've always wanted to do one of those.

Bequi and Carleigh are frozen in place, clutching each other for dear life as their piss commingles below them. A little impressed, but more so scared for their life. I turn to gaze at them, giving Bequi a little wink. Which was all the nudge she needed to run for the door. Right in front of the camera, like I had hoped. Before Carleigh had time to react and follow suit, I was already caressing Bequi's heaving lungs from the inside. The look of terror on her face invigorated me almost as much as the warm bath she sprayed me with while her insides cascaded down and out through the improvised opening I created in her tummy. With a big squeeze, I watch the life leave her eyes.

Bye-bye, Bequi.

That meant it was just Carleigh and I. My curly-haired little cheerleader, the apple of her father's eye. Even though she would only end up disappointing him when she came back home pregnant with failed grades. Don't worry, Carleigh, your on-again-off-again boyfriend would have been a deadbeat dad, and the kid was going to be named *Greece*. No, not like a nice way, grease of the bacon variety. Like the place, and no, neither parent was Greek.

Technically, I was doing the world *and* Carleigh a solid when I crushed her larynx in my grip and jerked her head from the fountain hiding just below her jaw in one fell swoop. All the TikTok audience saw was the sprinkling drops of red revealing the figure of a voluptuous woman, flirtatiously blowing them a kiss through the spraying crimson on my otherwise invisible form.

Share and follow for more, my little zombies.

I need to make a pitstop before I journey back to the office.

Chapter 7

She Had Me At "Arterial Spray"

I'm not sure if it's the leftover ghoul-endorphins or the ghoul-dopamine kicking in...*again, not going there*...but something has made me lose what little sensibility it seems I have left. I'm looking in Kyoko's bathroom through her shattered mirror. The glistening spiderweb was held in place with a big "X" duct-taped over it, obstructing my view. I transfer seamlessly to the floor-length mirror in her bedroom. Still no sign of her. Maybe she's downstairs. There are no other mirrors down there, unfortunately. She likes to get lost in her Animal Crossing town in the little nook between her living and dining room, so who knows how long until she comes back up.

Alright, so I definitely know more about Kyoko than I do about my typical summoners. Also, their "dossiers" are usually disposed of after their cases/body bags are closed. This situation is an anomaly in and of itself, regardless. I'm starting to rethink things. Maybe she'll be alright on her own. Maybe this was a false alarm, and I just overstepped. The thing is, I can't just phase in/phase out. My transfers leave a paper trail. The good news is, since this contract was opened but never carried out, it's up to the summoned to investigate and perhaps *finalize* their deal.

Just as I'm about to chicken out and transfer back, I hear the sound of someone approaching, and I hold my stagnant breath. Kyoko walks in, looking just as beautiful as before. Her rosy pink lips rival the slight swell around her eyes. It pains me to know she's still crying. I run through her thoughts as she readjusts the tie on her fluffy lavender robe and looks forlornly through the cracks in the mirrored surface. I sit back and hug the darkness, hoping for some kind of camouflage as I do my final *wellness* check on this mystery woman.

"I know you're there." The mousey voice I expected is instead throaty, pained, but strong. I'm thrown off guard.

"Wha-How?" I yell, trying to both mentally and physically catch myself.

Get it together, Mary.

"You just told me. I asked before, and you didn't answer." She steps closer to the maze of sharp edges and appears to be peering through the cracks. "This time it was different. I can feel when you're nearby."

Fuck. Fuck. Fuck. This is bad. All bad.

As if I wasn't already nervous, all this blowing up in my face—centuries of service going null and void—started to creep into my thoughts.

"Centuries? How old are you?" Kyoko asks, adding to my frazzled mind.

"One thing at a time, Kyoko!" I say, slightly below a yell in case it's hard to hear me through the thin crackles. I paused, hoping for some time to think.

"Why didn't you kill me last night?" she asked. The space between us stayed empty and silent.

"Because I-because you didn't finish the summoning."

"So if I say **Bloody Mary**-" she stopped in her tracks, her mind stuck in mental quicksand.

"It resets after a time limit. Don't say it again... just so my ass is covered."

My thoughts were doing the backstroke away from the sinking ship that was my brain. I lost count of how many protocols I just broke until one single thought breached the surface.

"Why would you want to kill yourself?" escaped my lips before I had time to stop them.

Tears streamed from Kyoko's beautiful, hooded eyes.

I knew I fucked up.

She sniffled.

"You didn't fuck up. I called you. You picked up. I just- I get so overwhelmed. Then I'm all alone, and I let the intrusive thoughts win."

Pictures of her with friends and family come to my mind like I was there to witness the festivities myself. I'm confused how someone so bright and lively could ever feel alone or unwanted in this world.

"I'm pretty good at masking. I've done it my whole life."

This whole mortal being able to read my thoughts should be bothering me more, but honestly, it just feels comfortable knowing I don't have to explain myself as much. I typically like to slash first and fill out the paperwork later, but this is a nice change of pace.

"Adopted. Lost in the child care system. Over-achiever. Shy by default. Came out as asexual. I was basically born to be alone and set myself up to stay that way."

"Wait, wait, wait," I say, trying to keep up with all this new information. My brain was still pro-cessing masking and asexual.

"Masking just means I can hide my depression very well. I put on a happy face until I get home and crash."

I grimace, knowing that feeling all too well, but just never knew how to say it.

"As for asexual, well...that just means I'm not interested in sex when it comes to relationships," Kyoko said, her voice softening as she opened up to me.

As the questions came to the forefront of my mind, she confidently answered.

"Sex is not off the table, but I'm not looking for it. I prefer romance and intimacy, something that...most of the people I've dated never fully understood."

This was not a completely new concept to me. I had just never heard anyone else put it into words before. I felt the same way, honestly, even before I officially disembodied. Sometimes I just wanted to feel close and comfortable with someone without having to get physical. Especially now because...well...mortals, or ephemerals if you want to get politically correct, tend to die when I get physical nowadays. The whole concept being laid out this way made it all click. Things just started to make so much more sense to me.

A relaxed silence fell between us, both staring through the glass back at Kyoko, when I remembered she hadn't actually *seen* me before. This had accidentally become somewhat of a one-sided blind date that neither of us actually signed up for.

"I won't lie…I'm curious to see what's so scary about you." Her sweet voice and the warmth emanating from where my pumping vital organs used to be vanquished what little common sense I had left.

"I won't turn to stone or anything, will I?"

"Oh, I'm not a gorgon, and if I were one, I would have mentioned I was Greek like six times by now. Trust me."

The sound of her cute little laugh made me grin. I can't think of the last time I made a joke.

Am I flirting with her?

She stopped and smiled before I panicked. I allowed her to see me through the spiderwebbed glass and waited for the shrieks of horror.

"No shrieks. No horror. I wish I could pull off black like that." She said, taking me in as I stepped closer to the illumination from her vanity lights.

"Wow, you're hot!" she said after a beat. I blanked, my thoughts not quite getting traction during all this. How is a little ephemeral flipping my world upside down? Making me nervous with a kill count of 60,031?

"That's very impressive. I'm not keeping you from any willing...or unwilling victims right now, am I?" she asked innocently.

I checked my phone.

"I just left a kill before I got here. I've earned some downtime, if you need to talk."

She pursed her lips and climbed up on her sink again, sitting on the counter next to the rippling mirror.

"I'd much rather hear about your last kill." She said, bunching her robe under her butt.

I hovered closer to her—to the point that we were shoulder to shoulder—just a thin sheet of broken glass between both of our smiles. An hour had passed between me explaining to her how kill counts work, how our summoners track, and how I left the Kappa Zeta Jones sorority a lot quieter than it was before I got there.

"Poor Lux. She sounded like some of the girls I'm in class with." Kyoko stops and stares off across the room. Her thoughts seem fuzzy to me.

"Yeah. Peer pressure accounts for basically eighty percent of my CSF's. Critical Success Factors. The rest is just...poor decision makers and adrenaline junkies." I say, stretching and yawning. Then what I just said dawned on me.

"Not that I'm calling you..."

Her thoughts cut me off while she's still staring off into space.

Kyoko thinks *I'll be all alone again when she leaves,* but she says, "It must be cool to just appear wherever you want to and kill with no remorse. To be an urban legend that's real, but anyone who sees you dies."

"Well, there are some loopholes," I say, glancing at her out of the corner of my eye.

Maybe I can use my final girl clause on her to get out of this?

"What's a final girl clause?" she asks, yawning and adjusting her position.

"Nope. It's your turn to tell me about *you* some more. The legal mumbo jumbo is the most boring part of the job. Trust me."

"Telling you more about me would just depress you. I'm warning you now." She says, snickering and looking in my direction.

"Try me."

By the time we got done swapping origin stories, comparing dating standards of now versus the 1600s, and her talking me into working a little pink into my wardrobe here and there...it had already hit one a.m. It felt like, with the lack of defenses or pretenses, we had somehow squeezed weeks of deep conversation into only a few hours. We shared thoughts that we had never known the other existed before this week, and how we were both grateful to know better now. I felt safe and secure without explanation, but I wasn't going to question it.

Kyoko had curled up on the plush Hello Kitty bathroom rug on her tiled floor with a black and white striped blanket she grabbed from her room. Even though I insisted she get in bed, she was a stubborn Aries, so I knew when to pick my battles.

"Can you stay until I fall asleep?" she asked innocently. "I miss just lying with someone-" she yawned and nestled some more.

That won't be too far off.

"I promise," I said, close enough to my side of the mirror to see my breath. *Again, if I had any.*

"I could tell you about the fraternity I turned inside out. I ended three bloodlines that night." I said with a smirk, watching Kyoko drift off.

She giggled and closed her eyes.

"Can you tell me that one tomorrow night?" She asked, letting out a silent little exhale.

"It's a date," I said, watching her drift off to sleep. Enamored by this strong little warrior whom I would eviscerate anyone for, even though she didn't need me to.

I popped the cap on my *vintage* lipstick and wrote

on the back of her mirror, for her to wake up to; before I blew Kyoko a kiss and reflected home with a big, stupid smile on my face.

Chapter 8

<u>You in Danger, Maaaary</u>

I woke up in a great mood, and not just because it was Thirsty Thursday and most of us go out for drinks after our shift. I slipped into my work ensemble, thinking about what other juicy endeavors I wanted to tell Kyoko. She made the cutest face that lit up while I told her all the gory details. Finishing up my makeup, I was about to reach for my signature shade of lipstick when I got inspired to try out something new today. "HeartStopper" was the brightest, bubblegum pink shade I owned. Kyoko would adore it.

I reflect into the lobby, on time somehow, considering I was too excited to sleep last night. Ingrid Cold, aka The Grinning/Smiling Man, was adjusting his suit and tie in the mirror, but let out a startled cry telepathically as I step past him. He looks me in the face, and his signature rictus fades as he creeps up on his work-husband—The Mothman. Few others in the lobby turn to stare at me. I nervously turn to inspect my reflection, just in case I got any sprites in my teeth on the transfer over or something. Awestruck, I'm greeted with the biggest, most horrifying smile stretched across my face.

"Morning, Mary," Olivia, the femme ogre, says as she gets in line. "Somebody's kill count must have hit double digits last night." She added through a plum lip and a toothy smirk. I felt my pallid face flush before I nervously joined the jovial green giant.

"You should have seen the other team," I said, allowing our shared giggle to release the anxiety. *I was in a good fucking mood, dammit. It was about time.*

"Damn straight!" said the Smiling Man, peering from behind the Mothman, both of them smiling back at me.

"Stop that, Ingrid!" I laugh, "Get out of my head before I relive the skimpy sorority babes I slaughtered last night just for you."

"Ew!" he shrieked, stepping through the security clearance. The line moved pretty quickly, even though I wasn't in a hurry. I checked the luster of my mercurial manicure when I noticed Pearl huffily get in line behind me.

"Morning Pearl," I say, buffing a bit of schmutz from my claws.

"Oh, what's so good about it?" Pearl said dryly, her mouth sounding extra wet and obstructed. The line advances as I inquisitively ask "Did ya patch things up with Brigitte?"

"Of course not!" She fired back, sputtering unintelligibly behind me.

Godfrey the Golem groaned at the front of the line. His dripping clay clogged the metal detector again. I turned to eye the clock when I caught sight of the aftermath of Pearl's barbed blowup yesterday. Her tanned, football-skin face hung in loose tatters off her skeletal bone structure. She continued to pat her powder puff of bronzer around the gaping holes her spikes had punctured through her pierced skin.

The line advanced, *finally*.

"It's not that noticeable, right Mar'?" Pearl said, through her constricted, drooping lips.

I hate when she calls me that, but I was determined not to let Pearl—or her perforated, presumptuous, prickly personality—rub me the wrong way.

"You've never looked better, Pearl," I say deadpan as I walk through the security scanners.

"Aww, thanks hun!" she exclaims, clasping her compact shut, jostling through the scanners.

The hell hounds won't stop staring at her loose, pendulous jowls, but she's too busy pulling her scalp back to see through her detached eye holes.

Even Cropsey's jaw dropped morosely at the sight of our cryptozoological equivalent to a Kardashian as she waggled past him, trying to catch up with me at the elevators.

The elevator dinged just as she caught up to me, unfortunately. She stepped inside as I hit our floor and fought not to roll my eyes.

"Did you hear about what happened after Sandra's thing?" Pearl said, carrying on her one-sided tea-spill. "We both got one month penalties each. No ephemeral reprieves for either of us."

I couldn't take my eyes off her ear, dragging down her neck from the weight of her blood diamond studs.

"So I can't even go see my guy to get all *this* fixed until then. It's such bullshit." Pearl said, her words sticking to the sides of her gnarled lips between slaps.

I winced.

"You went to an ephemeral plastic surgeon?"

"Well, I wasn't going to go to the Dread Doctors! Those fucking quacks. It took four surgeries just to fix the botched tummy tuck they did on me." She said peevishly as we departed the elevator and each other's company, thankfully.

"Mind if I borrow your stapler, Hun?" She asked behind me, through a preparatory gasp and a loud, wet sneeze.

I headed toward my desk and shuddered as I heard skin folds loudly slop and slough loudly behind me, amid Pearl's whiney blubbering. I pushed that mental image out of my head, determined to return to my good mood; thankful I wouldn't have to see her again until lunch.

Most of the office has been recovered. Sandra's celebratory kill feast didn't destroy too much of my side of the office, thankfully. I survey the damage, mostly to the carpets. Nothing gets kids blood out, trust me. Hopefully, they invest in a darker color next time. My desk had only shifted a few feet, which the Minotaurs in maintenance were more than happy to move back for me. While I waited for my PC to boot up, I glided to the break room to grab some coffee. Yes, let a ghoul have her one vice. It's all I ask for, really.

I'm waiting for the K-cup maker to perform its wizardry, brushing a stray baby tooth into the trash when Diego, the Wendigo, joins me. He raises his non-existent eyebrows in my direction before he opens the fridge. I return the eyebrow raise at whatever it is that we have a joint qualm with this morning.

"Can you grab me the creamer when you get a second?" I ask with a smile. A *grin* crosses his emaciated humanoid head as he nods and stares at his choices on the fridge shelves. Besides the three different half sheet cakes, there's a mixed berry yogurt —nearing its expiration date—or a snack bag of cut up toddler fingers. He hands me the creamer and begrudgingly grabs the yogurt before I hand it back to him. *Good for him*. He's a good guy. I love a strong, silent type, and he always smells so good!

I return to my desk, absent-mindedly thinking about tonight and doing my best to avoid the Basilisk's stare. Not because of the whole mirror thing. I owe Beatrissss Girl Scout cookie money. She is notorious for cornering her victims and putting the squeeze on them until they cough up their cash.

My PC is up and running, when I notice a dreaded flashing email notification marked urgent. My empty insides tighten as I finish off my coffee and click it. The Baba Yaga wants to see me, first thing. There went my good mood.

Leto's purple polkadot bowtie buzzed me in. I couldn't see the worried look on his face, but I know it was there. Baba was sitting at her grand desk, her eyes skimming her screens through her readers sitting on the tip of her crooked nose. She pretended she couldn't hear me come in. You know, the whole floating thing, but we both know she did.

"Masha," the chair nearest her desk slowly pulled out for me. "I think we have some issues to discuss, mayhaps, yes?"

No couch. No tea brewing. I'm fucked.

Baba's smile was warm, but her eyes were stone cold and unflinching.

"It has come to the department's attention that you have willingly gone against more than a few company protocols during the last week."

She rose, glancing at a suspicious-looking carved owl clock on her bookshelf I had never noticed, before returning a wide-eyed stare to me. My cold skin felt like it was about to ignite. I was doing my damndest to maintain my composure. Baba's nostrils flared, and she continued.

"These protocols were put in place for not only the safety and the efficiency of the company, but also to manage any risks or incidents that can occur to the deti."

"Baba, let me-" was all I got out before I felt my jaw lock and my death breath jammed in my pulsing throat.

The Baba Yaga exhaled and spun in midair toward her bookshelf. The purple folds of her sarafan continued to twirl until she landed, after grabbing a large dusty book off her shelf, and tapped the owl clock with her extended pointer nail. I barely noticed as I fought to move, noting the rest of my body was bound as well. She fluttered her eyelashes at me, then the oversized book hovered before her eyes, turning its pages.

"Otherworldly Paranormal Protocol # 345," she paused to lick her thumb, "no canoodling with ephemerals."

This is 2025, calling them ephemerals is problematic...probably, and someone actually approved the word canoodling in the policies and procedures manual?

Baba tutted and continued.

"O.P.P. # 499. In terms of Summoning Liquidations: Once the contract is initiated and conjuration has commenced, the summoned must complete the summoning, either by default or successful summoner exsanguination. The summoned is then to promptly initiate the appropriate kill sheet, clear their point of contact locale cache, and finalize all kill reports in order to claim a successful kill."

You lost ALL OF US after "O.P.P." Baba.

The Baba Yaga cleared her throat, then glared at me while the book flipped a few pages ahead.

"Pipe down, Masha." She muttered through gritted teeth.

THEN REMOVE THIS MUZZLING SPELL, WITCH.

Baba inhaled and let out a choked cough, looking at that damned owl and then me one last time.

"One Day of Ruination and one Final Girl clause allowed per six-month period." She paused, "Wrong section." The pages fluttered past her readers. "Ahh, O.P.P. # 677. Violation of company protocol may result in disciplinary action, which may include the loss of accrued credits against a termination technician's sanctioned afterlife reassignment stint."

Ok, that one even shut me up.

Baba sighed, replacing the book before vanishing in a puff of purple smoke and reappeared seated behind her desk. I held my silence and composure, mainly because I had no choice.

"Because this is your first major infraction, the department has agreed to consider this briefing your formal warning. Any further misconduct will be addressed with much harsher consequences, including dismissal from the sanctioned afterlife reassignment stint indefinitely, voiding all transmigratory advancement hereafter."

She pulled her readers from her face and folded them neatly in her hands.

"Are all my points clear, Mary *comma* Bloody?" Baba asked, as the motherly grin returned to her aged face. I couldn't wait for her to break the spell so I could tear her and this department to shreds. I waited for the feeling to return to my extremities, when I suddenly felt my head turn toward the bookcase, and my mouth began to move.

"Yes, I hereby agree to be bound by all terms and conditions of this After-Action Review," escaped my lips in an unrecognizable diction and cadence, concluding in an uncharacteristic toothy grin. I wanted to claw the entire building down to its bare bones.

The Baba Yaga nods just as my conjuration receiver chimes, indicating that I had a prospective summoning.

"Saved by the bell." Baba snarked. She raised her poised hand in front of her face. "But before you go, let me leave you with the wise words of an old friend of mine. Amor fati." Then she

snapped her fingers in a puff of sorcery sprin-
kles. Everything went black.

Chapter 9

<u>Who's Manning the Hot Topic?</u>

"I am Putressa, Mistress of Acid Baths and puncher of babies."

Where the fuck am I?

"And I am Lady Casketini, betrothed to Lucifer and hater of anything Lububu adjacent."

What the fuck.

"We are gathered here tonight to summon forth our accursed den-mother, she who reflects our true dark selves and helps us get our black eyeliner straight. **Bloody Mary!**"

That's two.

There's a group of gasps as my involuntary reflexes snap me out of my enraged brain fog. I feel my claws lengthening and my senses heightening as I stare up at a bunch of tweens who look like pale raccoons in Halloween make-up.

"Dumbass, you just said her name again. Caleb was supposed to do it." A voice angrily whispers in the darkened, candlelit basement.

"Whatever! We can edit it out later."

"Can we hurry this up? My mom is going to be home in an hour, and I still have to empty the dishwasher."

"Then fucking go, Caleb! Er, I mean Mortadello, Bringer of Profane Pronouns. Whatever."

There's a scoff in the room as I zero in on my conjurers.

"Avast Ye Mateys! For I am Mortadello! Bringer of Monstrous Insanity and xe/xem pronouns!"

"That's pirate speak, you simp."

My skin crawls. I really need these kids to just get this over with. I want them dead already.

"Oh fuck, let me do it again."

Melanie, aka Putressa, angrily turns the lights on, nearly tripping over her extremely long latex dress. Her prepubescent hips are barely covered by the cutouts. Her father is going to have a hissy fit when he has to identify the body.

Am I in a fucking mirrored coffee table?

"We have to start it again, and I have to pee anyway." She says, clomping out of the room in platform heels that she can barely maneuver. The clomps continue down the hall until a squeak and tumble can be heard. I can't help but chuckle a bit.

Caleb and Lady Casketini, aka Vanessa, are brother and sister. Caleb has begun transitioning and looks very dapper in xheir black jeans/black leather vest/dog collar combo.

"Then I go right?" says a boisterously effeminate voice belonging to Douglas, pulling his hot pink Hello Kitty hoody down around his middle. Poor kid hit his growth spurt right after his Grandma bought it for him for Christmas, and lost the receipt. Kyoko would love it.

Oh no, Kyoko. What the hell can I do? If they cleared my cache, I'd get nailed for even looking up her location.

Putressa returns, rubbing her skinned knee as she kills the lights.

"Ok, let's go," she says as she rejoins them, pulling up her milk crate to their coffee table altar.

Oh, these adorable little scamps. I almost wish I could take a picture before the carnage.

Mortadello hits record on xheir phone and joins xis three friends as they sit around the Ouija board. I let out an auditory groan and made sure they heard it before I reflected into the mirrored wall sign behind Putressa's dad's failed bar setup.

"OMG, did the mic pick that up?! Chat, I think we've made contact!"

"I think that was a Lord Montagay fart. I definitely smell an evil presence."

Oh, precious Putressa, you would have been a great Olive Garden Hostess. So full of vim and vigor, for the next four minutes at least.

"IT'S FUCKING RECORDING, FAM."

"I am Mortadello! Bringer of Monstrous Insanity and xe/xem pronouns."

"And I am Lord Montagay, master of sass and eater of *that*." Douglas delivers impeccably.

All five of us giggle.

Yaga gave me this assignment to distract me. I just know it. Damn that witch.

"We gather here to conjure our most gaggy blood mistress, to beg for her rizz and lethal prowess!"

They all place their hands on the planchette and rhythmically sway, rolling their eyes in the back of their heads. I'm getting antsy thinking about how in the hell I am going to be able to get a message to Kyoko.

"Spirits! Command chat to hit that subscribe button."

Putressa takes over.

"Spirits! Did McKenna White's dad actually say she would get a Tesla Truck for her Sweet Sixteen, or did she just make that up for clout?" She asks with a straight face.

"Whoa. You're moving it, Casketini!"

"No I'm not! My fingers are barely on it."

The planchette swivels around the board before landing on *YES*.

Lord Montagay laughs uproariously.

"OMG, how fucking tragic. Thank you for spilling tea, spirits!"

I didn't move shit by the way.

"Ask if Mr. Forgit really got Mrs. Walker pregnant!" Mortadello asks, wide-eyed.

Lord Montagay pipes up. "Girl, I can already tell you that's all cap."

The tweens break into a cacophony of inane nonsense words and numbers, including phrases that they are way too young to know the meanings of. I can feel a migraine coming on. Maybe I can try to reflect to Kyoko's school and reach her there without the department finding out.

C'mon kids. Please don't make me lose more faith in this generation than I already have.

"Fam! Stop it already, we're supposed to be conjuring **Bloody Mary**!" Putressa yells over the ruckus.

Sigh. Showtime.

A stony silence falls over the room as I extinguish all the candles but the one in front of the Ouija board. I float past each soon-to-be-in-memorialized-TikTok-account. I whisper their names in their ears, making the hairs on the napes of their little necks rise before

I reflect back into the coffee table. The tension builds as my lengthening claws scrape the back of the mirrored surface. Adrenaline makes for the best arterial spray.

I begin to move the planchette on the Ouija board, feeling the urgency coursing through my veins. The tweens are stupefied, leaning in to witness my magic show. I slow my movements until they get the hint to place their hands on the planchette and help Aunt Mary out for this part, for the sake of time.

"Holy fuck!" Mortadello whispers as the planchette travels around the board.

"Is this really Bloody Mary?" Lady Casketini asks.

My bloodlust is maxing out. It was time to crash this plane.

I moved the planchette to *YES,* and the room erupted in awestruck gasps.

"Do you have a message for us?" Putressa asked, staring at the recording phone.

I move the planchette again.

YES.

"I can't believe we're getting all this! Think how much monetization this video is going to get!" Lord Montagay whispers loudly.

The planchette swivels, and they draw nearer as the first word spells out.

Mortadello watched the planchette closely. "G-I-R-L. She spelled girl!"

"It's still moving! B…Y…E? Bye? Wait, she's leaving already?!" Putressa yells.

"GIRL BYE!" Lord Montagay exclaims. "Sis, I'm dead! She said Girl BYE! So iconic!"

My claws pierce the rippling reflection and send the Ouija board flying in the air. The kids can't take their eyes off it as it spins and the board shreds into pieces. Then I allow them and the camera to see me strike my best death dealer pose. I hate to pull a rushed ending, but these were dire circumstances.

All the mystified gasps are cut short when I fan out my claws, extend my arms, and give them my best 360. My perfectly executed fouetté caused all of their adorable little heads to pop off like marshmallows in a spray of blood around me. The gurgling spouts of crimson against my alabaster skin create the illusion of a grotesque baroque fountain while I execute a grand plié.

Candyman could never.

I let the spray absorb into me to give me enough juice to fuel this frantic scavenger hunt. I wish I had time to give 'em more of a show, but I had a date to get to that I wasn't willing to break for anyone.

I reflected to her school, checking all the places I felt her aura, but alas, no Kyoko. I was getting a bad feeling in the pit of my gutless gut the later it got. In between glimpses through art department lobbies and college coffeehouse restrooms, I couldn't help but think about this batshit insane situation I somehow got myself into. Even though Kyoko and I had just met, this felt like more than love at first fright. This felt deeper than anything my dead heart had ever felt, just in the night we shared. I knew answers to questions I hadn't thought to ask. She knew things about me that I never would have shared, even if you threatened me with holy water and a crucifix. This was a matter of life and death. This was worth risking my damnation for eternity in the ethereal nothingness. I reasoned I would at least get to see her one last time.

I scoured my mind while I reflected into my bathroom—trying to zero in on her coordinates since management wiped my conjuration receiver—as I gave myself a quick once-over coif. I was reapplying the pink lipstick when it hit me. I started to dig around in my purse and couldn't find my signature shade. I must have left it at Kyoko's. That could be my *in*, if I could just focus hard enough on it. I readied myself and prepared for what might be the biggest, happiest mistake of my afterlife. I needed to save the girl I...I just needed to get to her.

Kill Count
060,035

Chapter 10

Parting is Such Sanguineous Sorrow

I reflected into the mirror realm behind Kyoko's bathroom, which took a lot more out of me than I had expected. Now I remember why we switched to GPS after all. I find my elusive lipstick and pop it in my purse while I scan the room. It was pitch black and silent as the grave. I try and yell out to her, but my voice falls short in the dead space, with no reverb whatsoever. My stymied efforts register when I notice the broken mirror has been replaced.

My anxiety starts to spike as I reflect to Kyoko's bedroom mirror and am momentarily comforted by her glowing phone in the darkness surrounding her bed. The clock on her bedside table flashes eleven p.m. when it hits me how much time traveling without a known destination had taken me. Guilt floods my rotted insides. I see her shifting in bed, eventually getting up to go pee. I let her have her privacy, hoping I could somehow get her attention when she gets back. When she returns, I see through the brief light flash that she is wearing a cute black dress with pink fishnet stockings on. Her hair looks like it's bright pink and newly styled. *She did all this for me. Now I feel even worse.*

She heads downstairs, leaving her phone in her bed. She returns with a bottle of wine, and I groan. She grabs her phone and heads to the bathroom, bottle in hand. I transfer there as the light flicks back on before I start pounding on the glass. She doesn't react at all. She glances at her reflection, and I'm able to see her tear-stained mascara bleeding down like black dripping candle wax.

There's no way this mirror was fixed or replaced in that short amount of time. This has the stench of the Department all over it, I think, as the tears fill up my mirrored eyes.

"I'm here!" I scream, pounding on the glass. "Kyoko! Look at me! I'm here!" I continue, loud enough to feel the glass vibrating between us. I'm rendered powerless to speak to her in any way. My mind is reeling, but I'm all out of ideas. Blood-tinged tears flow down my face as my pulverized fists ache from the pounding.

Kyoko climbs up on the sink again, bottle and phone in hand. I experience the most unwanted deja vu as she sits with her shoulder closest to me. I mirror her pose, just like last night, praying to the Dark Lord that this contact would at least register something to her. She sets the bottle down next to her—where I am happy to see no other sharp implements joining her—and starts typing on her phone again.

From my vantage point, I could see her phone screen and the message she seemed to be typing as a note.

I HATE FEELING ALONE, YET IT'S ALL I'VE EVER KNOWN. YOU'D THINK THAT AFTER A WHILE, ONE WOULD LEARN TO ACCEPT THEIR OWN FATE. YET HERE I SIT, JUST ME AND THE MIRROR. I HAD A GLIMPSE OF HAPPINESS, BUT I SHOULD HAVE KNOWN THAT EVEN THE SUPERNATURAL WAS TOO GOOD TO BE TRUE. WAS SHE A DREAM? I SHOULD HAVE KNOWN BETTER. I WAS BORN TO LIVE ALONE, LOVE ALONE, AND DIE ALONE. WHY NOT HELP THE PROCESS?

"That's not true, Kyoko! Do you hear me!" I screamed through my tears. "Please just stay strong for me! I want to help you!"

She unceremoniously puts her phone down and grabs the wine bottle, taking a glug out of it before wiping her mouth and sobbing in her arms. I'm beside myself, shuffling through ways to break this curse and help her, but coming up blank with every scenario. Kyoko sniffles and lifts her head, wiping her nose on her arm before turning to look at me in her reflection.

"I just wasn't meant for this world, I think. I thought you felt the same way." She paused to take another swig. "Maybe cruel fate meant for us to meet, knowing it wouldn't last. Not on opposite sides of the pane at least."

I watch her lavender manicured nails feel around the sink, and my heart drops. Luckily, it's just for her phone.

I DIDN'T WANT TO DIE ALONE, BUT I THINK I FOUND A LOOPHOLE.

I'LL MISS YOU ALL.

I'M SORRY, I WASN'T STRONG ENOUGH.

XOXO,

KYOKO

I gasp as I read her final sendoff.

"**Bloody Mary,**" she says quietly.

My lifeless heart drops as my conjuration receiver dings in my purse. Warm blackness floods my eyes. I jump up and scream at her.

"STOP THIS KYOKO! THIS ISN'T WHAT YOU WANT! I PROMISE YOU!"

"**Bloody Mary,**" she repeats, pushing her things on the counter behind her and returning to the floor.

There is no option to reject or accept this conjuration. Whether it be the proximity or the doings of my disciplinary action, I can feel my bloodlust surging. As soon as my claws grow to their full length, I begin to shred and swipe at the impervious glass.

"NO KYOKO! DON'T DO THIS!" I howl, still blinded by my own tears.

The silence fills the room as I prepare myself for what is about to happen. The animalistic hunger within me is severing the wires to any rational thought right now.

She pauses to wipe the tears from her face and takes a deep breath.

Noooooooooo!

"**Bloody Mary**" she whispers, letting a smile twist her lips upward.

I shudder and exhale, feeling my body involuntarily pass into the room as if I am being pulled by the strings of a puppeteer. Our eyes meet, both exhibiting deep sorrow, as well as genuine excitement to see each other. My head fills with so many things I want to say to her all at once, but the thirst has taken over. I can't utter a single intelligible word. We are standing face to face at this point, her soft sobs the only sound in the heavy room. Her eyes are staring through me, understanding, taking in everything I want to say, but knowing it's still too late. Every muscle in my body trembles as I fight to hold the floodgate of my vicious urges back.

Kyoko nods and falls into me, entwining herself into me. It's the first contact I've had since I took my final breath. I never want it to end. I wrap my arms around her, taking her intoxicating cherry scent in so strongly that my nostrils burn. I've never felt a connection like this before. I'm lost in the moment. Like I'm flying for the first time.

Then I feel our feet dangling below us, and the reality that we were both floating hits me. Kyoko is still quietly sobbing and holding me tight. My temples throb as she pulls away and whispers, "I'm sorry it had to be this way."

Tears I didn't know I still had flowed as I gripped her tighter. Her eyes widen before her face softens into an agonizingly serene placidity. I am a feral beast lost in the deep, dark forest that is her embrace. I gently caress the pumping grooves of her beating heart. Her warmth spills down, cascading off my arms dribbling to the floor. I fight to hold her gaze. My body is a killing machine doing what it was programmed to do, without conscious command. Kyoko's breathing slows, and the beginning of a pained look washes over her face.

I hold her heart in my clutches as if it's my most prized possession—protecting it from the harsh world that she was forcibly born into—before I say "I love you" and shatter it before her dying eyes. Her final tear falls on my cheek as her body goes limp. I am left feeling unbearably empty and alone. I let the only constant I knew—the darkness—consume me.

Chapter 11

Surfing the Crimson Wave

I 've had a lot of time to ruminate on reverse-existentialism. Pondering the meaning and values in a purposeless afterlife was all I could do; before I found Sudoku. I knew the day I accepted my contract to become a Phantasmic Independent Contractor that I would be cursed to haunt the living, draining them of their life forces to keep my own light flickering until the next victim. Sounded good to me. I'm a Cancer. Where do I sign?

I had accepted that the end of my mortality would extend into my social life, but this was a blow that I hadn't anticipated. One of the first things they covered during orientation was to never get involved with any ephemerals. Especially not one who we were sanctioned to eviscerate. It had never occurred to me to even fathom shitting where I ate. Yet here I am. Wailing through the empty void, losing precious blood through my tear ducts, for a girl that I had only known for forty-eight hours. Tears that were most likely Kyoko's blood. Which just made me want to launch into another crying fit, knowing I couldn't. I needed to save my strength for tomorrow morning.

I pried my face from my coagulated, blood stained pillow and threw on the lone suit I had left in my closet. I haphazardly wiped my face and tried to look at least somewhat decent for my last day. I wanted to go out with a bang, but not looking crazy in case the security camera footage would be used later if this went to court. I sighed as I wiped the last of my coagulated, teary snot away and looked back at my apartment. It would probably be the last time I saw it, so I was trying not to get even more choked up. You'd think I'd be better at goodbyes. I take in a sigh of resignation and collect myself before I reflect through to the Department lobby.

I rocketed through the security check queue, ready to gore any friend, foe, or colleague who dared to get in my way. To my chagrin, the line parted as I darted through the security checkpoint. I even got the nod from the Hell Hound. I didn't have time to overthink the situation. I quickly reflected into the mirrored walls of the opened elevator, which seemed to welcome my speedy vengeance as well.

Even the muzak was making me angry as much as my thoughts cycled, keeping my rage simmering.

I'm glad the guy who wrote "Tis better to have loved and lost than never to have loved at all" was nothing but maggot-food now, because he couldn't be more wrong. I know there's no way to reverse time, but if the department hadn't intervened, there was a chance I could have saved her. If I didn't quit,

I would have been terminated regardless. My time here was done. I've done the unthinkable and fallen for an ephemeral. Not just an ephemeral, a living, breathing ethereal creature that humanity didn't deserve. I couldn't plague this realm knowing her face would torment my thoughts from now until "retirement."

I dabbed the last drip of hemoglobin from the corner of my eye before the elevator doors opened and my fury resurrected. I bolted out into the lobby, startling Circe, who clucked in indignation. The bright pink *Welcome* banner threw me off, but my vexation pushed me through. Mordrake was absent-minded, walking through the hall that led to our sector as I flew past them. His better half saw me coming and sibilantly whispered, "You'd be prettier if you smiled," eliciting a hissed response from me.

"Fuck your life coach bullshit!" I propelled past them with enough force to knock them against the walls. "Where's Yaga?!"

Edward yelled back in his husky voice, "In her office!"

I continued to our sector, unfazed by the rest of the floor being put back together, nor the gathering of my coworkers around a table of refreshments; all it was missing was another damned cake.

"Baba Yaga!" I shrieked, startling the ravenous horde from their store-bought charcuterie mid-chew. The throng of Imps and Boogeymen/women parted, except for Pearl. She had just taken a bite out of some summer sausage as I halted in front of this detached, bad-built obstruction. The clearance bin Barbie looked unfazed, with her face still hanging off of her gleaming white skull like an oversized pet sweater.

"Pescatarian my ass, you raggedy-faced episode of Botched! Just give it up already. You don't need a plastic surgeon, you need some guts and a shotgun!" I screamed, causing her to shudder and run for the restroom in tears with bits of flesh flaking off her.

I felt all my wrath building up like a plastic explosive ticking between my ears. Detonation was imminent, and in the name of my new and improved laissez-faire attitude, I decided letting the inevitable happen was the only rational panacea. I let the eruption consume me, unleashing hell itself with a scream more powerful than I had ever thought possible. Every reflective surface in the office shook and crackled, allowing droplets of crimson to dribble from the cracks. My throat ached, but I continued my infernal shriek. I pulled every ounce of energy I felt emitting from my ravaged heart, before I evoked Kyoko's smiling face that first night. Everything went red.

Computer monitors, window panes, and even the convex mirrors covering the floor cameras erupted in deluges of blood. The force of the torrent reached the tops of the cubicles, lifting and shifting all the office furniture into the frothing swell. The few coworkers who kept their heads above the crimson waves looked displeased, to say the least. Sandra sailed past, giving me a manicured thumbs up as her monstrous tail propelled her toward the elevators, taking the crimson tide with her. I bet the guys on the second floor will get a kick out of that.

The penny-scented space fell silent as a few employees shakily rose from the puddles. Baba Yaga's door opened. The esteemed witch emerged with her feet planted in her cauldron and her broom in hand as she entered the fray. Her eyes looked to me, blood-caked and claws flared; then to the dripping ceiling and the disheveled office.

Chapter 12

The Girl of My Screams

"Masha. In the future, we ask that you give at least 24 hours' advanced notice before a day of ruination." She paused before she looked to her left. "Loot?"

Her invisible secretary piped up, "Yes, Miss Yaga," from behind his desk that was now on its side and three feet to the right.

"Please make a note that Mary, comma, Bloody has been briefed on company policy this quarter," said the Baba Yaga in no particular direction.

"Consider it done," the blue bow-tied nothingness responded back.

"And tell Janitorial they better put on some coffee."

Baba turned to me and smiled sweetly.

"Feel better now, Masha? Sometimes it's good to just get it all out."

I was debilitated, basically speechless after what—I am pretty sure—was my first plasmic tidal wave. I could barely stand, let alone focus on the speech I had prepared and run through my head most of last night.

I took an exhausted step closer to her, trying to pull my residual hate into my throat. When I tried to speak, my lips formed words, but my spent vocal cords only emitted a sound somehow lower than a whisper.

"That's probably for the better, Masha. We wouldn't want you to over-exert yourself."

My face twisted into a portrait of pain and anguish, powerless to this all-knowing witch.

She raised her eyebrow and gave me an omniscient grin before she exclaimed.

"Well, if no other issues need to be addressed."

I keened in frustration.

"Let's welcome our newest addition to the Department."

The Baba Yaga stepped aside, letting hot pink and purple wisps of smoke crawl across the floor. I dropped to my knees in awed anguish.

"Everyone say hello to Kyoko, part of the Yōkai Division. Our first Ungaikyō!" Baba Yaga exclaimed, giving a golf clap as the enchanting ghoul entered the space.

Most of the employees had returned, in much higher spirits, in order to celebrate their new comrade. They all clapped and yelled excited words of encouragement.

"I guess it's good we left the cake in the fridge," Baba said, smirking and moving towards the break room.

Kyoko beamed. I couldn't take my eyes off of her. Her black kimono was highlighted by hot pink accents that seemed to breathe along with her as smoke enveloped her bone white skin. Her beautiful features were defined by sharp black and red liner, coming to points bordering her face. Her signature pink hair was replaced by long pieces of moving inky blackness, held in place by purple kanzashi sticks.

I still could not believe my quaking eyes.

Kyoko hovered over to me, on the verge of tears herself as she offered me her hand. I couldn't grab it quick enough. Our touch brought back the warmth and the connection we had that first night, tenfold. I stood, still flabbergasted, as I fought to string together any series of coherent words that came to my mind.

"I didn't want you to think I ghosted you," was all that came out, unfortunately. She responded with her signature giggle. Her reflective eyes stared fervently into mine.

"Deep down inside, I think I knew the truth," Kyoko said. We stood hand in hand. "I guess fate just had different plans for us," she added, smiling and nodding toward the Baba Yaga, returning with a pink cake box floating in front of her.

"Finally, someone who gets it," Baba added with a smirk, setting the cake box down and letting it unfold for its unveiling.

The cake read:

I was getting choked up as my foresight of our future together played in my head. Kyoko lengthened a single claw and excitedly sliced her cake into perfect square pieces.

Baba Yaga laughed and laid the cake knife back down on the table.

"I guess that works too." She tutted. "She's like a kid with a new toy, this one!"

Kyoko giggled and grabbed us each a piece of cake. (Bless her heart.)

"How did you know red velvet was my favorite?" Kyoko asked Baba as we picked a dry spot near the busted windows to catch up.

"Oh my sweet child, I know everything. Just you wait and see."

The festivities carried on for most of the work-day. No Conjurations came in to train Kyoko, but Monday was another day, thankfully. She got introduced to everyone on the floor. Even Pearl, who agreed to let bygones be bygones. She knew it was *just the anger talking*, she offered, truly believing that. The Baba Yaga apologized to Kyoko for Sandra's hasty departure but said the two of them would have a full sit-down once she got back from the Kaiju Conference she was speaking at across town.

It felt like I had so much to fill Kyoko in on, yet I didn't. Even after a few uncomfortable ramblings, she silently told me the eight most calming words I think I've ever heard on this side of the grave.

"We have all the time in the underworld."

Damn, and she was new at this?

Gnomatic tech support had to get her in the system and set her up with the basics, so Baba thought it would be the perfect time to call me in to her office. I was reluctant but knew it was inevitable. I had memorized this walk of shame more since *you've* met me than I have in my entire afterlife. I guess love makes even the most seasoned executioner act out of their infallible nature. That was what I planning to lead with at least.

Chapter 13

Score One For the Dark Side

"**A**h, my precious Masha, please come in." The Baba Yaga cantillated, as her floating settee scooped me up and brought me to her, sitting poised at her desk.

Oh Brother.

Baba grinned and tapped her steepled pointer nails together to the tune of *May There Always Be Sunshine.*

"Tea, my dear? Perhaps some ginger and lemongrass would help you replenish after such a strenuous... incident." She said with a hint of venom on her tongue. I turned to check for the lone owl clock on her bookshelf, but noted its golden eyes were uncharacteristically closed.

She smirked and tapped the side of her bumpy nose.

"That sounds lovely. You know I'm always receptive to your graciousness." I say, with a half-hearted grin on my face.

"I was counting on that, actually," Yaga said, rising from her desk.

"While I am pleased that the circumstances worked out in all of our favor, Masha. The Department cannot risk these haps to stance again."

She tented her fingers—the way they all taught us to during orientation—when you wanted to rip someone's throat out but couldn't.

"This old brain of mine. I'm struggling to remember how those torch-yielding puritans in HR taught us to respond to this type of situation." She paused, "...ah, yes. This was identified early on as a likely outcome."

She cleared her throat and stared at me.

"So I'd appreciate my...shared insights being better considered on future decisions, perhaps earlier in the process to help mitigate potential risks," Baba added with a smile that showed every tooth in her mouth's possession.

I slowly blinked and did my best to hold my smile.

This...witch.

"I'll be sure to give that a try next time."

A whirring sound caught my attention. I noted the owl clock's golden eyes gleaming and spinning in place.

"Like music to my ears." The Baba Yaga fluttered her eyelashes.

She continued, "And I think the best way to ensure the best outcomes for all parties involved...about my previous proposal..."

A scroll magically appeared before me and unfolded itself, until the signature line of the lengthy contract bowed before me. A quilled pen appeared in my hand.

"It's all very standard, Masha. Your sector is growing and could use a manager for future growth and succession. What's a few more responsibilities, more coins in your pocketbook, and a much-needed strong female in charge—to lead by example?"

The Baba Yaga obligatorily paused and waited for my reply. I weighed my options.

That's a lot more responsibility to take on, but it's a position I basically already did without thinking. I had so much more to look forward to now that the company had interred Kyoko. It didn't take clairvoyance nor Gremlin Data to foresee that fate had much happier plans for both of us. Just the thought of our future together be-stilled my idle heart.

I nicked the inside of my hand, enough to let a pool of blood fill my palm before I brought the pen to fill its reservoir. Baba grinned intensely as I brought the pen to the floating papyrus and swirled my crimson mark.

What's another notch on my soul when I've got someone to spend the rest of my damned eternity with?

<u>The End.</u>

(Until Monday at least.)

Stay tuned for more tales from the cursed cubicles of D.I.L.F. in the near future, Dark Lord willing!

Hey, that's me! So this is officially my fifth book in under two years, which still seems foreign to me and weird to say. I'd like to think that I prioritize quality over quantity, but even I'm like "Ok gurl, maybe slow that down some then."

I truly believe I had this festering ball of chaotic energy taking up space in my head. It wasn't until I discovered people may want to read the fucked up things that my brain comes up with; when it's bored or not wanting to perform the executive functions that I beg of it. So if you made it this far, thank you for reading my nonsense and allowing me to transcribe what the voices tell me, to the best of my abilities.

P.S. Remind me to make more of these little mini-bominations; for those who don't necessarily have the attention span to read 300+ pages of hot lesbian sex and blasphemous body horror. *cough* Scissor Me Timbers *cough*

Acknowledgements

I keep my circle small because I'm a classy dame like that. The few who are in my inner circle tho:

-the ones who get a random screenshot of absolute foolishness that I just wrote

-the ones to whom I send my half-done cover concepts featuring boobs to

-the ones who keep feeding the bedeviled machine that is my brain via compliments/praise that I'm afraid to give it. (What if he becomes more powerful?!)

-the ones who love and care for me, knowing the nightmare factory that resides behind my whimsical, otherworldly, ***mephistophelian*** grin.

-the ones who read the little pieces of me that I publish as books; that I force onto the world, one social media post at a time, whether they like it or not.

-the ones who look different, love different, think different; whether you embrace it or not. You are my people, and I see you. Never change, because imagine how depressingly boring being *normal* must feel. Ugh, bring a book. *cough*

I appreciate you all and thank you for allowing me to do what I love! Pissing my parents off, er, I mean...inundate the world with the horrors that it so assuredly deserves.

xoxo,

Phrique

To delve into the mind of Phrique, you better have some boots on. You're going to encounter much fuckery, such foolishness, but the only gratuity you'll get from him is his flippant use of blood & gore. His horror elements are always with intention. As deliberate as his use of hyperbole, allegory, euphemism, *punnery*, & words he just made up on the fly. Life has no guarantees but if you're reading Phrique, know you're in for a treat. If you like it subversive, sardonic, transgressive, all while being tongue-in-cheeks throughout: you need some Phrique in your life. Don't take his word for it, ask your dad.

Https://linktr.ee/phrique

www.ingramcontent.com/pod-product-compliance
Lightning Source LLC
Chambersburg PA
CBHW071430300726
48976CB00004B/1288